PINK MAGIC

by Donna Jo Napoli
Illustrated by Chad Cameron

Clarion Books
New York

Clarion Books
a Houghton Mifflin Company imprint
215 Park Avenue South, New York, NY 10003

The illustrations were executed in collage and acrylics.
The text was set in 18-point Orange.

www.houghtonmifflinbooks.com

Manufactured in China

Library of Congress Cataloging-in-Publication Data

Napoli, Donna Jo.
Pink magic / by Donna Jo Napoli ; illustrated by Chad Cameron.
p. cm.
Summary: Nick wishes for some pink mail addressed just to him, and his sister helps make it happen.
ISBN 0-618-15985-1
[1. Brothers and sisters—Fiction. 2. Letters—Fiction.] I. Cameron, Chad, ill. II. Title.
PZ7.N15Pi 2005
[E]—dc22   2004012324

ISBN-13: 978-0-618-15985-7
ISBN-10: 0-618-15985-1

SCP 10 9 8 7 6 5 4 3 2 1

Nick and Pinky were telling each other stories on the porch when Mr. Moon came by.

"Hi, Nick. Hi, Pinky."

They peeked inside his mail pouch. "Did I get anything?" asked Nick.

"Sorry. Not today." Mr. Moon patted Pinky on the head.

Nick frowned. "Eva gets mail. Today's her birthday."

"Tell her Happy Birthday from me. It must be hard seeing your little sister get all those cards. How about you and Pinky deliver these letters to your mom? That'll be fun." Mr. Moon touched the tip of his hat in farewell and went on his way.

Nick tucked Pinky under
his arm and marched the
bundle inside to Mamma.
Mamma climbed down
from the ladder. She sorted
the letters and handed Eva
an envelope.

6

"Yay!" Eva ripped it open. "Another birthday card." She skipped around the room, waving her card.

"Who's it from?" asked Nick.

Mamma leaned over Eva. "It's from Uncle Bob. He can't make the party. See his little note? It says, 'I love you, Eva, even if I can't be there.'"

"Everybody gets mail but me," said Nick. "I want to get something in the mail. Something great. And pink." He hugged Pinky.

"You will," said Eva. "On your birthday."

"I can't wait that long," said Nick.

Later that day at the party, Eva squeezed
her eyes shut and made a special wish. "I wish
for Nick to get great mail," she whispered.
"Great pink mail." Then she blew as hard as
she could. Every last candle went out.

The next morning Eva and Nick and Pinky were eating toast and jelly on the porch when Mr. Moon came.

"That looks good," said Mr. Moon. "A picnic breakfast." He held out a stack of letters. "Who wants to deliver these to your mom?"

"Me." Eva grabbed the stack. "But isn't there anything else? Maybe something for Nick?"

"Let me check again." Mr. Moon searched in his pouch. "Amazing." He dug his hands down inside and pulled out a watermelon.

"Is there a card?" asked Nick.

Mr. Moon knitted his brows. "I don't see one."

"It's pink inside," said Eva. "And Nick loves pink."

Mr. Moon thought for a minute. "Well, then, you might as well have it. Watermelon's perfect for a picnic."

"Wow," said Nick. "Thanks."

Eva twirled her way into the house. "Melon, melon, melon," she sang. "Pink, pink watermelon."

Nick rolled the watermelon behind her.

Mamma put her hands to her cheeks. "A watermelon? Where did it come from?"

"Mr. Moon brought it," said Nick.

"Mr. Moon the Mailman? Isn't he sweet."

They picnicked in the backyard and grinned watermelon grins.

The next day Nick and Eva and Pinky were drinking watermelon smoothies on the porch when Mr. Moon came.

"Hey, kids." He smiled and held out the mail. "Here's today's stack."

"Anything else?" asked Eva. "Maybe something pink?"

"There can't be a stray watermelon every day," said Mr. Moon. But he looked inside his pouch anyway. "Now, what do you make of that?" He eased out a flamingo.

"Yay!" said Eva. "That's even better than a watermelon."

"Is there a note with it?" asked Nick.

Mr. Moon checked the flamingo's neck. "Nope, nothing."

"It's pink," said Eva, hopefully. "So it must be for Nick."

Mr. Moon sighed. "Well, I guess if someone else on my route tells me they were expecting a flamingo, I can always come back and get it from you."

"Thanks!" said Nick.

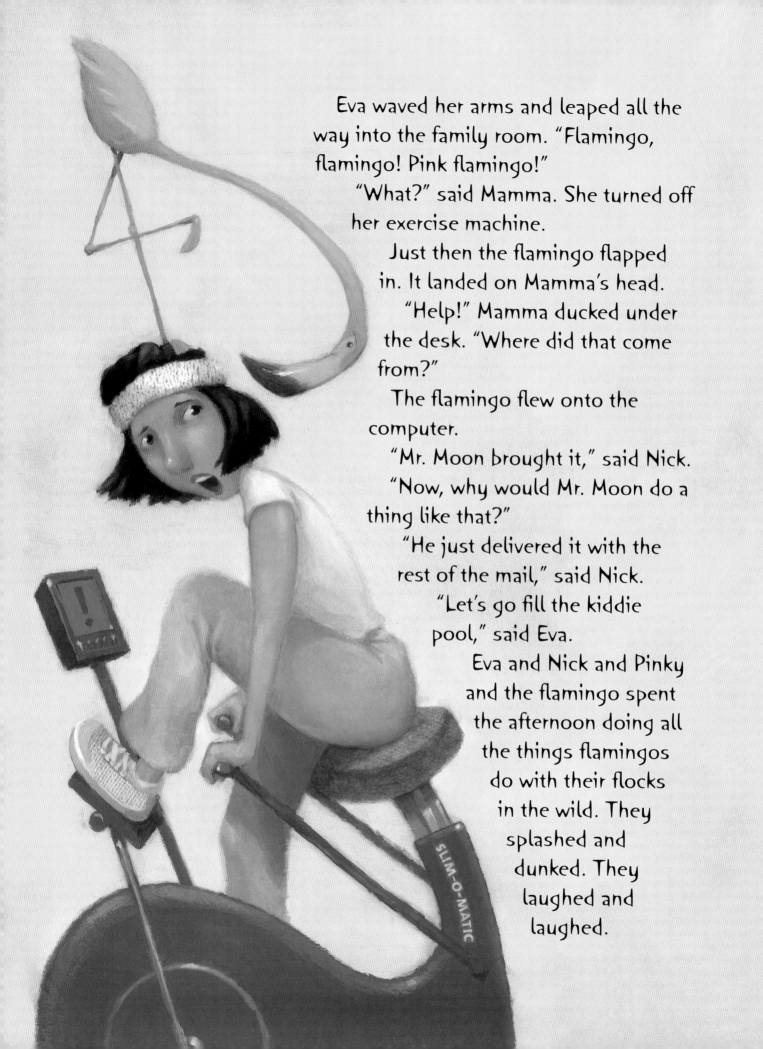

Eva waved her arms and leaped all the way into the family room. "Flamingo, flamingo! Pink flamingo!"

"What?" said Mamma. She turned off her exercise machine.

Just then the flamingo flapped in. It landed on Mamma's head.

"Help!" Mamma ducked under the desk. "Where did that come from?"

The flamingo flew onto the computer.

"Mr. Moon brought it," said Nick.

"Now, why would Mr. Moon do a thing like that?"

"He just delivered it with the rest of the mail," said Nick.

"Let's go fill the kiddie pool," said Eva.

Eva and Nick and Pinky and the flamingo spent the afternoon doing all the things flamingos do with their flocks in the wild. They splashed and dunked. They laughed and laughed.

The next day Eva and Nick were coloring on the porch when Mr. Moon came.

"Hey, nice colors," said Mr. Moon.

"Shh." Eva pointed at Pinky and the flamingo. "They're sleeping."

"The flamingo ate our shrimp dinner," Nick whispered.

"Oops," said Mr. Moon.

"No, we're glad," said Nick. "We hate shrimp."

"We love the flamingo, though," said Eva. "All except Mamma. She said to tell you we don't appreciate this kind of mail."

"Well, maybe she'll like the flamingo more when she gets used to it," said Mr. Moon. He held out a stack of letters.

"Are you sure there's nothing else?" asked Eva. "Nothing pink?"

"Let's see," said Mr. Moon, taking another look in his pouch. "Well, I'll be . . ."

A snout pushed its way out. Then another.

"Pigs!" said Eva. "That's the greatest thing yet."

"Is there a card that says who they're from?" asked Nick.

Mr. Moon shook his head. "There's no room for anything else. If this keeps up, I'm going to have to get a bigger pouch."

The passel of pigs chased each other around the porch and woke up the flamingo, who honked and honked.

"They're pink," said Eva.

"So they're yours," said Mr. Moon.

"Thanks a lot!" said Nick.

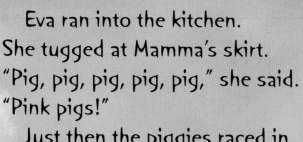

Eva ran into the kitchen.
She tugged at Mamma's skirt.
"Pig, pig, pig, pig, pig," she said.
"Pink pigs!"

Just then the piggies raced in.

"Eek!" Mamma dropped her stirring
spoon. "Mr. Moon again? What's gotten
into him?"

Pigs snuffled through the garbage bag under
the sink. They ate the magnetic letters off the
refrigerator. They leaped onto the chairs and
knocked over the fruit bowl on the table.

"Out!" shouted Mamma. "Out, out, out!"

The pigs ran out the back door, with the
flamingo flapping above.

Eva and Nick and Pinky and the flamingo spent
the rest of the day

balancing hoops for the
pigs to jump through,

blowing whistles as the
pigs raced in circles,

and holding nets while the
pigs did acrobatics.

Finally, Nick and Eva sprawled on the ground, exhausted. The piggies came up and ate their shoelaces.

Nick kissed Pinky and sighed loudly.

"What's the matter?" asked Eva.

"All this mail," said Nick.

"The watermelon was sweet."

"Yup," said Nick.

"The flamingo eats anything we don't want."

"Yup," said Nick.

"The piggies are even better than a circus, 'cause they're never over."

"Yup," said Nick.

"You wanted great mail," said Eva. "And look what you got."

"This is good mail," said Nick. "But it's not great. Remember the birthday card you got from Uncle Bob? You love him and he loves you. That's great mail."

That night, when Nick fell asleep, Eva picked up Pinky. She held him to her ear and listened well.

The next day when Mr. Moon came, Nick gathered up the flamingo and put it into Mr. Moon's pouch. Then Eva helped him tuck in the piggies.

"Sorry," said Nick, "you have to take them back. Mamma says no more animals. Of any kind."

"Too bad," said Mr. Moon. "You looked like you were having fun. Well, here's the mail." He handed the letters to Nick.

Just then a giant pink elephant trunk popped out
from the mailman's pouch and flopped onto the porch.
Without a word, Nick and Eva and Mr. Moon
pushed the trunk back into the pouch.

29

When Nick and Mr. Moon weren't looking, Eva slipped something else into the pouch. Then she tugged on Mr. Moon's shirt. "I think there's something else in there," she whispered. "Something meant for Nick. Look again. Please."

Mr. Moon bit his bottom lip and blinked. He opened the pouch just a little and checked once more. "Why, there is another letter, after all. And the envelope is pink with a big N printed on it." Mr. Moon scratched his head. "N for Nick, I bet."

"Really?" Nick put the rest of the letters on the porch floor. He opened the envelope. "Oh," he breathed. He pointed to the drawing. "That's Pinky."

"He wrote you a letter," said Eva. "It says, 'You're my best friend. I love you.'"

"That's great!" said Nick. "I got a letter from someone who loves me." He looked at Eva. "Someone I love, too."

Eva laughed. "You got something great in the mail. And it's pink, pink, pink," she sang.

"Well, I guess that's the end of that," said Mr. Moon.
He turned to go.

They heard a soft peep.

"What's that?" asked Eva.

"It's coming from your pouch," said Nick.

Mr. Moon tipped his pouch, and a baby chick hopped
out onto his palm. "I'm going to Bruce's house next,"
he said with a shrug. "He must like yellow."